TINY TIMMY

SOCCER SUPERSTAR!

A Scholastic Australia Book

To Kyah Tim Cahill,
my first baby, who introduced me
to the fun of kids' books.

Scholastic Australia
345 Pacific Highway Lindfield NSW 2070
An imprint of Scholastic Australia Pty Limited
PO Box 579 Gosford NSW 2250
ABN 11 000 614 577
www.scholastic.com.au

Part of the Scholastic Group
Sydney • Auckland • New York • Toronto • London • Mexico City
• New Delhi • Hong Kong • Buenos Aires • Puerto Rico

Published by Scholastic Australia in 2015.
Text copyright © Scholastic Australia, 2015.
Text by Tim Cahill and Julian Gray.
Illustrations copyright © Scholastic Australia, 2015.
Illustrations by Heath McKenzie.

National Library of Australia Cataloguing-in-Publication entry:
Creator: Cahill, Tim, 1979-
Title: Soccer superstar / Tim Cahill; illustrated by Heath McKenzie.
ISBN: 978-1-76015-888-0 (paperback)
Series: Cahill, Tim, 1979-. Tiny Timmy; 1.
Target Audience: For primary school age.
Subjects: Soccer–Juvenile fiction. Soccer players–Juvenile fiction.
Other Creators/Contributors: McKenzie, Heath, illustrator
Dewey Number: A823.4

Typeset in Mozzart Sketch and Bizzle Chizzle.

Printed by McPherson's Printing Group, Maryborough, VIC.
Scholastic Australia's policy, in association with McPherson's Printing Group,
is to use papers that are renewable and made efficiently from wood grown in
responsibly managed forests, so as to minimise its environmental footprint.

10 9 8 7 6 5 4 3 2 1   15 16 17 18 19 / 1

CHAPTER 01

'**I**s that **the best** you can do, **Tiny Timmy**?'

I got up and rubbed the mud out of my eyes.

It sure wasn't easy being the **smallest kid** trying

out for the **SCHOOL SOCCER TEAM**.

Hacker called out again, '**Is that <u>ALL</u>**

you got?'

His pal Studs piped in, 'Yeah, are you trying

out for **swimming** or **soccer**?'

Flip the
pages to
see me
in action!

Hacker was **big** and **mean**. Studs was **small** and **sneaky**. Neither of them was very bright, but they did have a point. I'd been spending **a lot** of time in the **MUD**!

Most of the kids at the tryout were able to

 **push me**

off the ball

easily.

My buddy **Mike** passed me the ball. Me and Mike have been **friends for ages**, and he was one of **the best** players on the team last year.

This was my first time trying out, and I **really** wanted to get on the team so I could play with Mike and my other friends.

I controlled the ball, looked up and set off on a **dribble**. This was my **last** **chance to impress** Coach Roach, so it needed to be good. I could see Hacker and Studs up ahead. I was sure I'd get past them this time, just like I'd imagined: I'd **run** up to Hacker and **dink** the ball through his legs, then **hop over** Studs's outstretched leg and **bang** the ball into the back of the net.

Coach Roach would see what I could do and he'd put me in the team **for** **sure**.

I'd p<u>robabl</u>y be

'Great tackle, Millie, clean as a whistle, lass!' Coach Roach's **LOUD** Scottish voice snapped me out of my daydream. I looked down and the ball was gone. **Millie** had stolen it off me and raced away. Did I mention there were **girls** trying out too?

'Nice one, Tiny Timmy, save your dribbling for your dreams!' said Studs.

'Yeah, dribble the ball, not down your shirt!' said Hacker.

I didn't feel **too** worried about what Hacker and Studs had to say. **Nobody** really worried about what Hacker and Studs had to say. But that didn't stop them from **saying lots of stuff!**

Later when Coach Roach posted the team for this week's game on the **NOTICE BOARD**, my name wasn't on it. Well, that's not exactly true—my name **was** on the sheet, next to **'orange boy'**.

LIONS' GAME DAY TEAM

Goalkeeper:	Liam
Defenders:	Studs
	Hacker
	Jonas
	Sienna
Midfielders:	Millie
	Nico
	Mike
	Kash
Forwards:	Ibrahim
	Cruz
Reserves:	Evie
	Tibor
	Bek
Cheer squad:	Kem
	Anna
	Tyson
	Holly
Shirt washers:	Noah
	Madison
Orange boy:	Tim

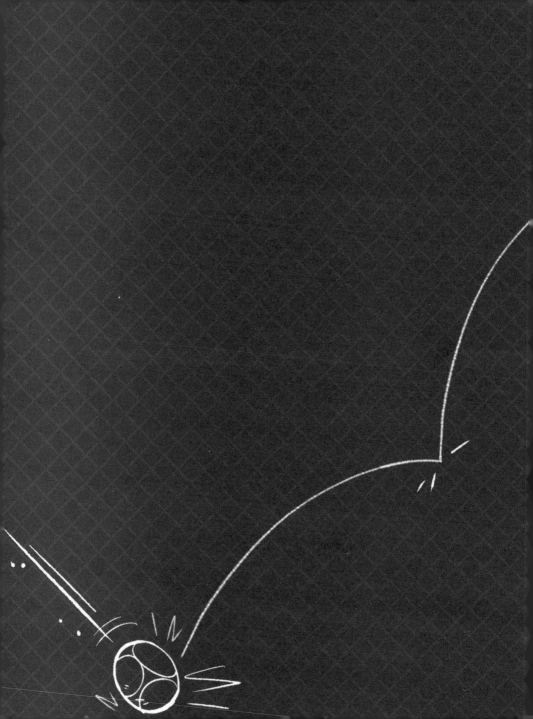

CHAPTER 02

I went to see **Coach Roach**. He was moving bottles, cups and cans around on his desk, **mapping out formations** for the team's first game.

He was **ALWAYS** thinking about soccer, even when he should have been doing other things. Like right now, when he was supposed to be teaching maths.

'Timmy,' he said, 'what can I do for you?'

'Coach Roach, I was just wondering why I didn't make the team?'

'Well, you are on the **"GAME DAY TEAM"** —oranges are **very important** for half-time energy replacement–'

'No, Coach Roach,' I said. 'Are you able to tell me why I didn't make the eleven? Or even get a place on the bench?'

Deep down I already knew the reason why, but then Coach Roach let me know for sure. 'They don't call you **Tiny Timmy** for no reason. The other lads and lasses are able to get the ball off you a bit too easily. You're **just not big enough** right now to play on the team.'

This was **bad news**. There was <u>**NOTHING**</u> I could do to **get taller** fast enough to get in the side.

'A **word of advice**, lad,' Coach Roach said. '**Practise** until you can't practise any more. Work on your game. You may not get any **bigger**, but you'll definitely get **BETTER**. Then who knows, it might not matter how big you are.'

CHAPTER 03

I took Coach Roach's advice on board. I would **practise** before school, at school, and after school until it was dark.

I'd **practise** all weekend.

I'd **practise** **passing** in the playground . . .

dribbling in the dining room . . .

and **keepy-uppies**

in the canteen.

Mike and I had also decided to do some **research**.
Maybe there actually *were* ways I could get **taller**,
and **fast**!

'What did you find out?' I asked Mike on the way
home from school.

'I've heard that if you **drink lots and lots of
milk**, your bones get stronger and longer and before
you know it you've **grown** ten or even **twenty
centimetres**!'

'Cool,' I said, and gave him a high-five. 'I've read that
if you do **lots of s-t-r-e-t-c-h-i-n-g** you
can grow up to **fifteen centimetres** practically
overnight.'

'**Wow!**' Mike said. 'If you try one of those, there's
a chance you'll get taller soon enough to get on the
team!'

I shook my head. 'Even better—I'm going to try

BOTH at the same time!'

That afternoon I put the **PLAN INTO ACTION**.

First I measured how tall I was and recorded my height

on the '**Tiny Timmy to Tall Timmy**' graph.

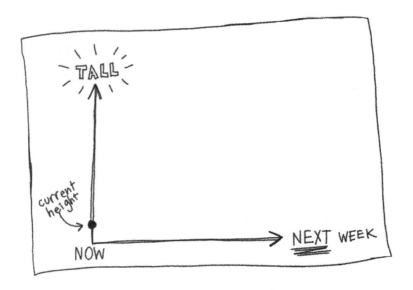

Then I ran to the fridge and poured myself a **big glass of milk**.

Then **another**.

And then **another**.

I felt **full**, but **no taller**. So I went back to the fridge and took out a new bottle, opened it up, and **drank it all** down.

Time for **<u>PHASE TWO</u>**.

I went out into the backyard and **jᵘmped up** to grab onto the fence. I bent my knees and hung on, **s - t - r - e - t - c - h - i - n - g** my muscles and bones as far as I could, but I still wasn't feeling any taller.

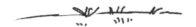

So I hooked my legs over the top of the fence and **hung upside down**, arms **out-s - t - r - e - t - c - h - e - d** reaching for the ground. I *still* didn't feel taller, but I did feel a **rumbling in my tummy**.

I was starting to regret **ALL** that milk I drank . . . and before I knew it, it all came **hurling back out my mouth**. And then it started coming **out my nose**!

To make things **worse**, through the spray of milk I saw Studs on Hacker's shoulders, peering over the fence taking pictures with his phone.

This would NOT be good!

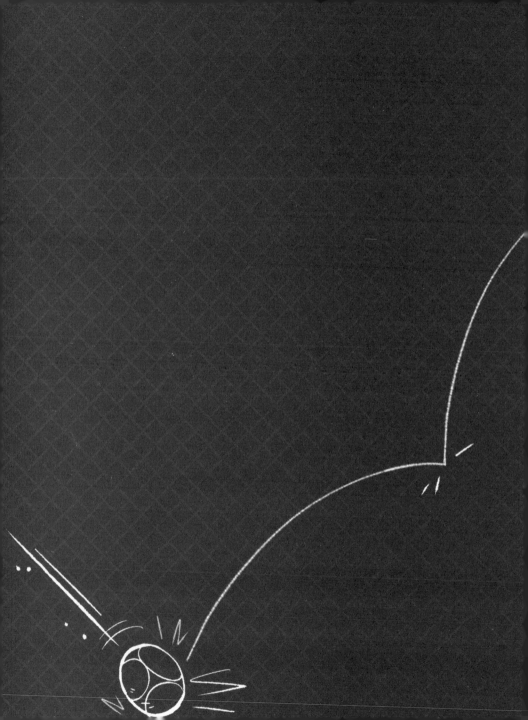

CHAPTER 04

was right. School the next day was **NOT** much fun.

It started as soon as I sat down in class.

'Hey, Tiny Timmy, how many Weet-Bix did you have today?' asked Hacker.

'He didn't have any,' said Studs. **'No milk!'**

'Yeah, it's all over his backyard!' said Hacker.

The kids in class **laughed**. They must have seen the picture that Studs took!

NOooo!

Then Mike showed it to me on his phone.

'**Nobody** cares what those guys say, Tim,' Millie said. She was another one of my **best friends**–and a really good midfielder, too!

'Yeah, I know,' I said.

It *was* actually kind of a **funny** picture!

But this wasn't even the worst part of the morning.

I had measured myself before school and **I hadn't even grown a millimetre**. It had all been for **NOTHING**! I'd have to think of another way to get taller and get on the team.

Time was **ticking**, and I was as far from **TALL** ↑ ↑ as I had been yesterday:

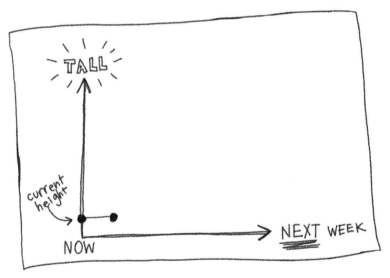

I wasn't happy with my flat-lining graph, but I still had a few **tricks** up my sleeve . . .

At lunch, Mike and I were **practising** passing the ball to each other.

'I can't believe the **s-t-r-e-t-c-h-i-n-g** and **all that milk did nothing** to make me taller,' I said. 'It's lucky I've heard of something else that should make me grow: **SLEEP!**'

'But everyone does that, and not everyone is tall,' Mike replied.

'True, but I'm going to **sleep A LOT!**'

'I know something that will help you get to sleep, fast,' said Mike. '**Warm milk**.'

'That's just **N<u>OT</u> funny**,' I said.

CHAPTER 05

There was no way I'd be able to get to sleep early without being **tired**. So after school, I ran straight out into the backyard, ready to do some **dribbling drills**.

'Hey, Tim!'

It was my brother **Shae**.

'Can I play?' Shae was younger than me, and he wanted to be a soccer player, too. He could at least go and get the ball if it went over the back fence. And **most** importantly, he was **smaller than me**!

So I said, 'Sure, we can play a practice match.'

'And you'll need a **goalie**, bro!'

That was my older brother, **Kyah**. He was

goalkeeper on his team, and was always keen to get

some more practice. He came out and set himself up in

goal, between the **clothesline** and the **rose bush**.

'DON'T YOU HURT
MY ROSES!'

I needed to tire myself out, so **I played <u>hard</u>**.
I **dribbled** around Shae. I **took shots** at goal. I
missed the target a lot, and Kyah saved nearly
everything else. But it was **good practice**,

and in the end I was **worn out!**

'Alright,' I said. 'Goodnight.'

'But it's **only four o'clock**,' Kyah said. 'You can't go to bed yet!'

I did need rest if my plan was going to work, but he was probably right—it was a **little bit early** for bed.

To fill in some time, I wrote a MATCH REPORT.

MATCH REPORT

The game was fast paced, but not many goals were scored. Tim showed good speed and his dribbling skills are improving.
His shooting was not so good, and Shae had to go next door six times to get the ball.
Kyah did well, only letting in one goal when Mum told him to let one in, just to be nice.

Shots taken — 16
Shots on target — 5
Goals — 1

It was **still** early, but if I needed **lots of sleep** to **grow** **taller** I had to go to bed now. Tomorrow was **GAME DAY** for the team, and if I wanted to be something other than **orange boy**, I needed to be **Tall Timmy** sooner rather than later.

I went to my room, shut the curtains, tied a sock around my eyes to keep all the light out, and went to sleep.

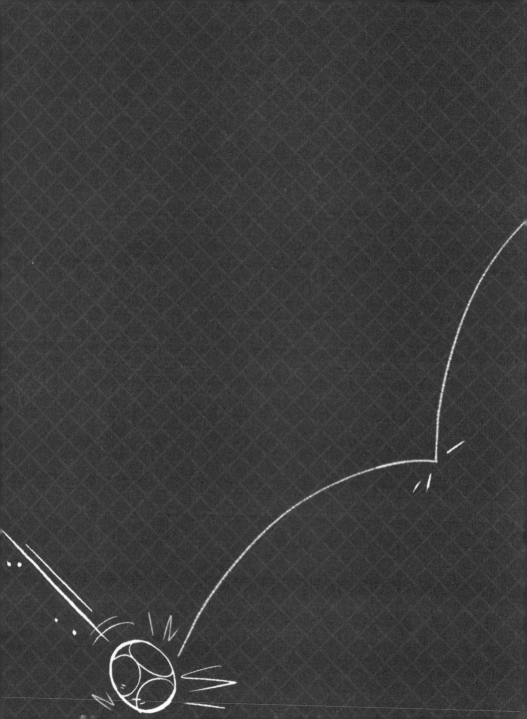

CHAPTER 06

When I woke up the next morning, the house was quiet. I felt like I'd had a **really good sleep**, so I ran off to see how much I'd grown.

'Whaaaat!'

I yelped. 'Still no change!'

If anything, I'd gotten

shorter due to a **bad**

case of bed hair.

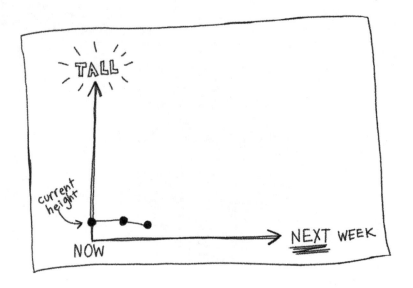

There was another problem. Where was everyone?

I needed to get to the game!

'Hello?!' I called.

Kyah was the only one around. 'What's up?' he asked.

'Where's Mum? Or Dad? I need to get to the field!'

'They took Shae to his game. They said to let you sleep 'cos you aren't playing today.'

'But I'm orange boy! Oranges are **very** important for **half-time energy replacement**! I still need to be there to help the team.'

'Well, you're **way late**, bro. You've been sleeping for ages.' Kyah pointed to his watch. 'That practice we did yesterday must have **really** taken it out of you.'

I couldn't believe the time. **I'd been asleep for HOURS!** If I left now, I might just make it for half-time—really the most important time for orange boys. I didn't want to let the team down.

But how would I get to the field? It was just at the end of our street, but our street was kind of long. Plus I had to carry a **huge** bag of oranges!

'Can you walk down to the field with me?' I said.

'Sorry, bro, Dad told me not to leave the house. Anyway, I'm getting picked up soon to go to my game. Tell you what, I'll watch.'

'What do you mean?' I said.

'I'll come out and make sure you get to the field OK,' he answered. 'I can watch you walk

➡ ➡ ➡ **all the way down there**.'

So off I went, lugging a **big bag of oranges** down the street. Kyah's an **awesome** brother, but I think he thought this was **a bit too funny** . . .

The walk to the field wasn't so bad. It actually seemed to **get easier** the further I walked. I must be **getting fitter**, with all the training I'd been doing!

I walked up to the sideline just as the ref blew the whistle for half-time.

The team looked **totally exhausted** ...

They'd be **all over** these **oranges**!

'How are we going?' I said to Mike.

'We're getting smashed, **3-NIL**,' he replied. 'Hey,

where are the oranges?'

'What do you mean? They're right—'

 Down

the

street

between

≥THE FIELD≤

and

MY

HOUSE!

The bag had an **orange-sized** hole in it!

There was only **one left**! No wonder the bag had felt

lighter the further I walked. It actually *was* lighter!

To top things off, Studs's **scruffy dog** was

slobbering all over the oranges.

The guys **weren't** going to like this . . .

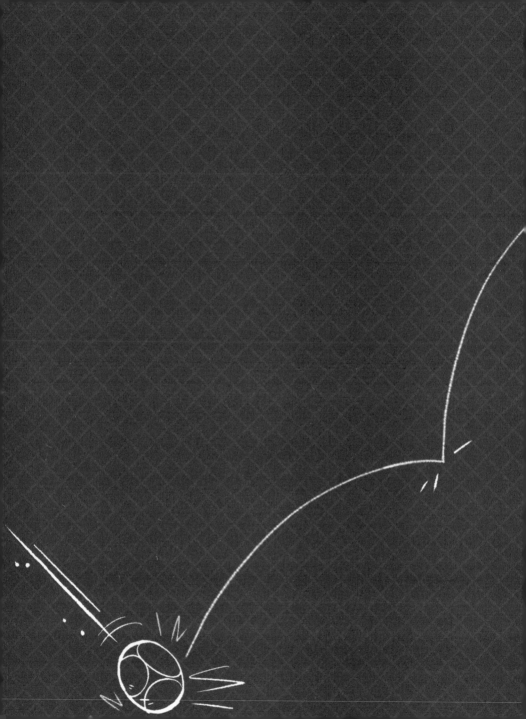

CHAPTER 07

'So, Timmy, you're telling me everybody gets **one piece** of orange for half-time energy replacement.' Coach Roach didn't sound **angry**, exactly, but he didn't sound all that **happy** either. He just stared at the one orange I had left, which I had separated into as many pieces as I could.

'Well, yes, but there's **only TEN pieces**, so two people will have to **share** a piece,' I explained.

'I was looking forward to that **juicy goodness**,' said Hacker.

'Yeah, you had **ONE job**, Tiny Timmy,' said Studs. 'You're not fit to be orange boy.'

I felt bad for the team, but was **secretly happy** that **Hacker** and **Studs** were the ones who had to share the one piece of orange.

'Right, Timmy, let's make sure you're here **early** for the game next time, and with more than one orange— **everybody** has a role to play in a **successful** team,' said Coach Roach.

Next time? I thought.

Next time I'd be on the pitch, **taller** and **better** and **READY TO PLAY**!

It got **worse** for the team after half-time. Our opponents, the **REDS**, ended up beating us **5-NIL**. It was only the first game of the season, but we would need to get **a lot better** to compete with teams like them.

Coach Roach spoke to us after the match. 'They were **too good** for us today,' he said. 'But there's plenty of improvement left in this side. Keep working on your skills and we'll **close the gap** on the Reds in **no time** at all.'

We all looked at each other. We weren't sure we'd ever be **good enough** to beat the top teams.

'I'm going to single one of you out,' Coach Roach went on. I was relieved because I knew he **couldn't possibly** be talking about **me**.

'Timmy,' he said, and looked my way.

Whaaat?!

I didn't even play today. More oranges wouldn't have made *that* much difference, **would they?!**

'This lad is a **great example** to you all,' Coach Roach said. 'He's not in the eleven, not yet, but I've seen him practising passing in the playground, crossing in the corridors, and keepy-uppies in the canteen. One stray kick knocked off my cap, but he's trying his hardest to **get better**.'

The rest of the team looked down at their boots. Most of them knew they could be **working harder** on their games.

I was glad that Coach Roach had noticed how hard I was trying, and that I was <u>serious</u> about getting in the team. All I needed now was to grow a few centimetres **taller**.

Surely that wasn't **too much** to ask?

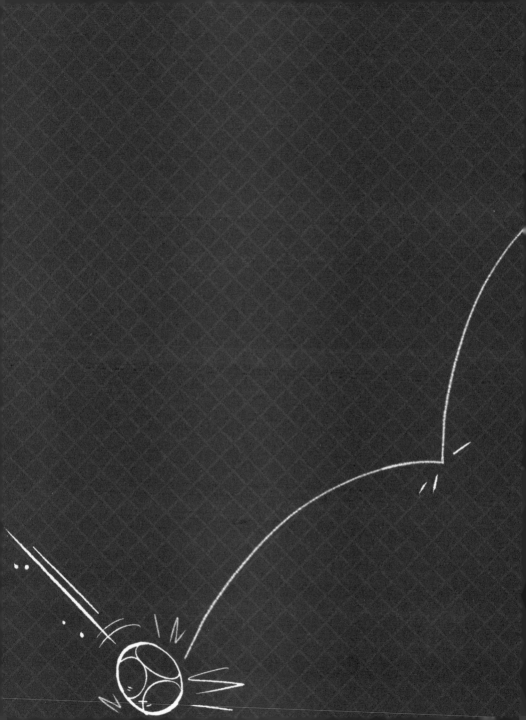

CHAPTER 08

Walking home after the game, Mike asked me how much I'd grown after my big sleep.

'Not one millimetre,' I said. **'Can you believe it?'**

'That's no good,' he said. 'What else can you try?'

'Well, I'm going to give it one more night. These things take time, after all.'

'Fair enough,' Mike said. 'Hey, can I come over and play a practice game with you and your brothers later?'

'**For sure!**' I said.

I looked over my shoulder and noticed Hacker and

Studs were walking home from the game, too. 'There's

Studs's dog again! He looks **mean and sneaky**,

just like Studs.'

Just then, the dog came **racing** up the footpath towards us, **yapping** all the way. I didn't want to get bitten, as that just wouldn't work with my heavy practice schedule. But there was **nowhere to go**! I had a **HIGH WALL** fence on one side, a **row of trees** on the other, and a **crossroad** just up ahead.

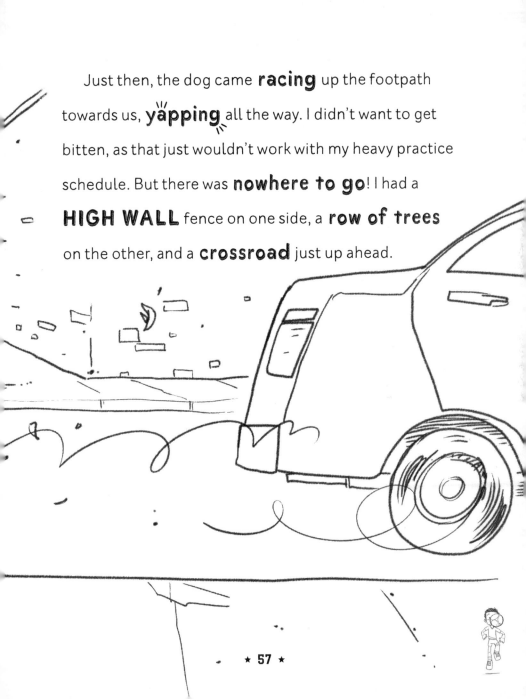

I could hear Studs calling from down the street. 'Slider, come back!'

That was a strange name for a dog, but I was more **worried** about how I was going to stop him from **biting** me.

Slider kept on **running** and **yapping**. What could I do? With Slider about to reach me, I looked over to the fence and **crouched down low**. I closed my eyes and used all the **power** in my legs to **jump up** and try to catch the top of the fence, and drag myself out of bite range.

Except when I opened my eyes again, I was standing

on top of the fence, **looking down** on Slider,

Studs, Hacker and Mike.

'**Whoa!**' exclaimed Mike. He walked over to

where I was standing, reached up and lifted my feet one

at a time to look closely at the soles of my shoes.

'What are you doing?' I asked.

'Checking your shoes for **sp⌊ings**!' he said. **'That was AMAZING!'**

'What just happened?' said Studs.

'I was getting away from your dog,' I said. 'He was about to **<u>bite</u>** me!'

'Slider just wanted to thank you for those oranges you "left" for him back on the field,' Studs explained. 'I was calling him back 'cos you didn't deserve any thanks.'

'Not after we had to share **one lousy piece**,' added Hacker. He mumbled something else about **'juicy goodness'**, before Studs went on again:

'But what just happened with you jumping **on top** of that fence?! I've never seen anyone **jump** anywhere near that high. Especially someone your size.'

He looked like he couldn't believe it.

I couldn't believe it myself!

'Anyway, don't get any ideas about getting on to the **SOCCER TEAM**,' Studs continued.

'Yeah, you're still **Tiny Timmy** to us,' Hacker said, and walked off with Studs and Slider.

'Hey, Studs, why is your dog called "Slider",' Mike called out.

'It's short for **"Slide Tackle"**,' Studs said over his shoulder, like that made it any less strange a name for a dog. Those guys really were **all about defending**!

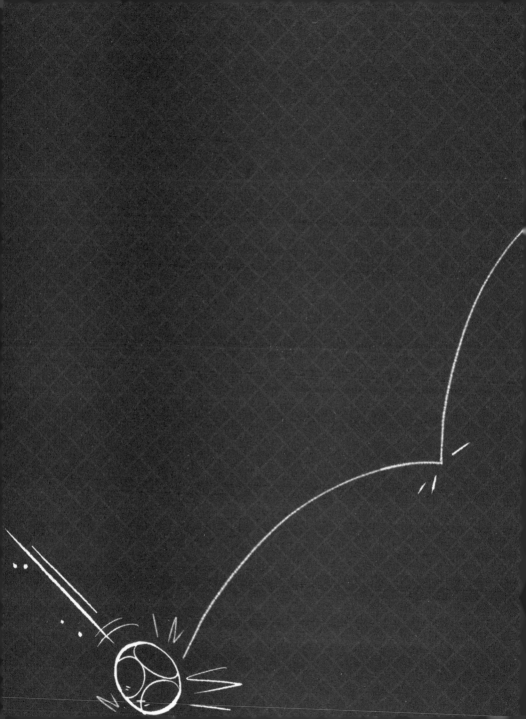

CHAPTER 09

'Show them, Tim. Show them how **high** you can jump!'

Mike, Kyah, Shae and I were in the backyard, ready for our next **practice match**.

'Go on, show them,' Mike said again.

I **crouched** down, then **sprung up** with all the ≥**power**≤ in my legs. I got up **high**, just like before, and seemed to **hang in the air** for ages!

'**Bro!** How did we not know you could do this? How did **you** not know you could do this?' said Kyah.

'I've never really tried. Well, at least, I've never really had to. I thought that dog was going to **bite me**!'

'Well that dog has done you a **big favour**,' Kyah said. 'Do you know what this means?'

'Umm, not exactly . . .' I admitted.

'It means you can **jump** up and **win headers**! **Score goals. Assist goals. Defend your goal**. This is a game changer, bro!'

Mike added, 'You're going to be able to jump higher than defenders, and get up even higher than some goalkeepers' arms. You'll get on the team now, and be our **SECRET WEAPON**!'

The only problem was, I hadn't practised headers much in the past. Sure, now I could j**u**mp high, but when I tried to head the ball, something was **a bit off**.

The ball **hit my nose**, or the **side of my face**–

Sometimes I **completely missed it**!

The other parts of my game were coming along well, because I'd been practising them a lot, but this heading would need **some <u>work</u>**.

MATCH REPORT

Before play even started Tim had worn himself out from jumping, due to repeated requests especially from Shae. Mike's passing was very good, Shae is getting more comfortable on the ball, and Kyah had more to do this time, but was strong again in goal.

Tim's dribbling is excellent, and his shooting was much more consistent. His heading needs to improve, but he's getting in good positions.

Shae still had to go next door three times to get the ball, but at least this time Tim could tell him exactly where to find it.

Shots taken — 14
Shots on target — 9
Goals — 3 (Tim 2, Mike 1)

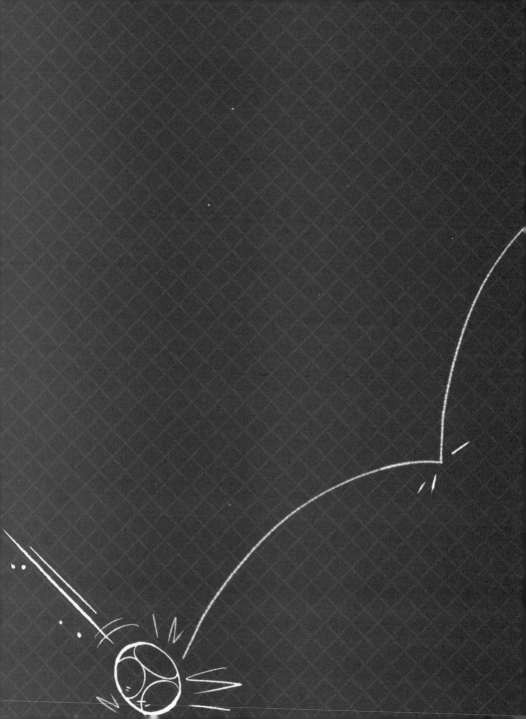

CHAPTER 10

Next morning, after another **extra-long** sleep, I measured my height.

No change, again!

This **sleep-more-and-you'll-get-tall** idea just wasn't working. I'd even given it two whole days and nights! The line on my **'Tiny Timmy to Tall Timmy'** graph was looking a lot straighter than I hoped it would.

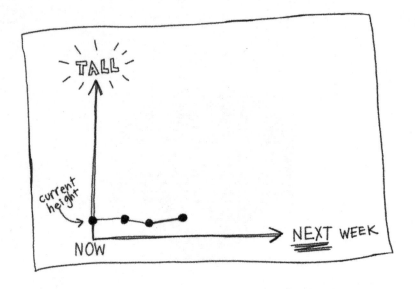

Although I wasn't getting any taller, I could at least

still **prăctise**.

It was the weekend, so I went down the street to the

soccer field with my brothers and Mike for another game,

this time on a **full-sized pitch**. Dad and Mum came

along, too.

MATCH REPORT

Tim's all-round game continues to improve. His shooting is getting more accurate, and his left-foot shots are getting stronger. The timing of his headers is getting better. His leap is still amazing. Once his technique improves, he will be unstoppable. Shae is also improving, and he was happy that he didn't need to go and collect the ball, because Dad was standing behind the goal. Both Dad and Mum are happy that we are at the park and not ruining the back fence and the garden. Mike's crossing is fantastic. Kyah's goalkeeping is still good, but he let more goals in because the goals are wider on a real soccer field.

Shots taken – 18
Shots on target – 12
Goals – 6 (Tim 4, Mike 1, Shae 1)

When we'd finished playing, I told Mike what I was planning to do tomorrow to get **tall**. Soccer practice was before school and Coach Roach was going to be blown away! No more **orange boy** for me, I'd be on the team next week!

'I don't know if that's a great idea,' Mike said after I'd told him my **brilliant new plan**.

'It's pure genius!' I said. 'I'm going to be **Tall Timmy**, literally overnight!'

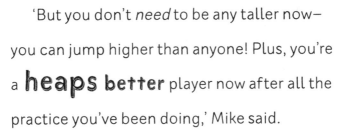

'But you don't *need* to be any taller now— you can jump higher than anyone! Plus, you're a **heaps better** player now after all the practice you've been doing,' Mike said.

'I know, but Coach Roach said I was **too small** to get on the team. And it's not much good being able to jump high if my headers don't go where I want them to,' I replied. 'This is going to be worth it, you'll see, but you can't tell anyone. **IT'S TOP SECRET!**'

When my alarm clock rang early the next morning,

I **jumped** out of bed straightaway. This was it. I

got dressed and ready for practice, then went and

measured myself.

'**Woohoo!**' I shouted. 'Finally!'

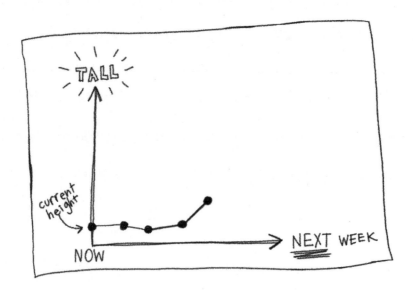

I was four centimetres taller, and it had been **easy!**

I met Mike outside for the walk to school. He looked at me and said, 'Are you sure about this?'

'If this **doesn't work**, nothing will,' I replied.

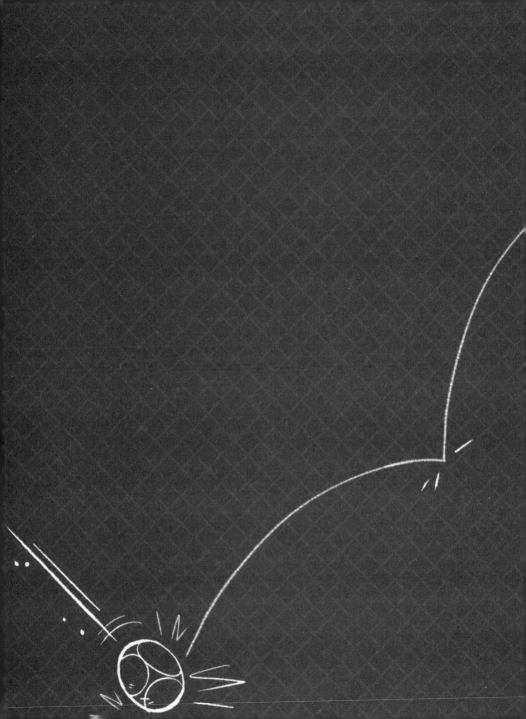

CHAPTER 11

It was crunch time.

SOCCER PRACTICE.

I was **taller**, my graph said so, now all I had to do was **impress** Coach Roach!

After our warm up, Coach Roach said, 'Let's start with some **passing drills**'. Everybody find a partner and pass the ball to one another. Start close and move a few steps back after each completed pass.'

Me and Mike started passing to each other. So far, so good.

Then Studs, who was next to us, passing with Hacker, said, 'There's **something different** about you today, Tiny Timmy. What's going on?'

'Nothing,' I said. 'I *am* feeling a **LOT** taller, though. I don't think anyone will be ➡ **pushing** me off the ball today.'

'We'll see about that,' laughed Hacker. 'And hey, how come you're wearing tracksuit pants?'

'Yeah, you **too good** to wear shorts like everyone else?' added Studs.

'Enough chatter, lads,' said Coach Roach.

'**Concentrate** on passing the ball.'

Mike and I moved another few steps back from each other. As our passes were getting longer, I was needing to put more **oomph** into each kick. And I was starting to get a **little bit wobbly** on my feet.

'You **OK** there, Timmy?' asked Coach Roach.

'No problem, Coach Roach,' I answered.

We moved back a few more steps. I was really needing to take a **big kick** at the ball now to get it down to Mike. It was my turn again. I **trapped the ball**, **knocked it**  **forward** a little, **took a few paces** and then

 **LET FLY**.

'TINY TIMMY'S FOOT HAS FALLEN OFF!'

shouted Hacker.

'That's not his **foot**, that's his **boot**,' said Studs. 'I knew something was different about you. Your boots are **too big!**'

It was true. This morning when I got ready, I put on **my** boots as normal. Then I put my feet inside **Kyah's** boots and laced them up.

That's when I went and measured myself.

It didn't matter **HOW** I was **taller**, just as long as I **WAS taller**. Nobody needed to know! At least, that's what I thought.

But now **everybody knew**. What would the team think? What would Coach Roach think?

'That was **quite a stunt**, Timmy,' Coach Roach said. 'What were you thinking?'

'You said I needed to be **taller**,' I said. 'This way, I **WAS taller**.'

'I also said if you **practised a lot** and **developed your skills**, it might not matter how tall you are. And everyone can see how hard you've worked and how your game has gotten better.'

'And you should see how **high he can jump!**' said Mike.

'Go on then, let's see it,' said Coach Roach.

I shook off Kyah's other boot. Mike tossed a ball at me, **high**, and from a standing start I **leaped up** and put my head to the ball. It hit me on the nose, but I was **way up in the air**.

'That is some **b**o**unce** in your boots, boy!' said
Coach Roach. Just like everyone else who'd seen me
jump, he was stunned. 'How did we not know you could
do this? How did you not know you could do this?'

'Well, I was chased by Studs's dog, Slider, and I
thought he was going to bite me, and–'

'Never mind, Timmy. If you can leap like that,
and play how I know you can play, then
you have a role in this team. You
deserve it, lad.'

I looked around, and everyone
on the team looked **happy** for
me. Well, everyone except for Hacker
and Studs. **Why were they so
against me!?**

CHAPTER 12

When practice was finished, Coach Roach called me and Hacker over.

'Hacker is the **best header** of the ball on our team,' Coach Roach said. 'Yes he's **big**, but he's doing **one thing** that you don't do, lad.'

Coach Roach tossed the ball to Hacker, who **headed** it back powerfully,

 straight into his arms.

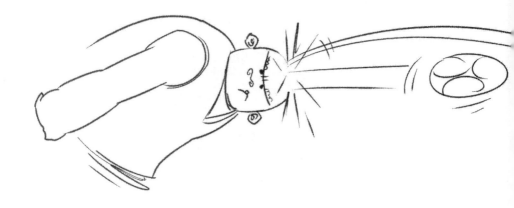

'You have the **spring** in your heels, Timmy, more than I've ever seen. You're getting in the right position. You're using your legs and your arms to get up high. Just one problem: **you need to open your eyes!**'

'Tiny Timmy might be able to **jump high**, but it's hard to see in the dark,' said Studs, who had appeared from behind a tree next to Coach Roach.

'Yeah, too scared to keep his eyes open,' said Hacker.

'That's enough out of you two,' said Coach Roach.

'Timmy's **not afraid**, anyone can see that, he's just

not had enough heading practice.

Give it a go, lad, eyes

wide open.'

Coach Roach threw the ball to me, head height.

Eyes open, I **headed** it  straight back. He threw it

higher so I had to **jUmp** to head it. Same result. Again

and again. I was making good contact with the ball and it

was going **just where I wanted it to go!**

Break-through!

Next, Coach Roach kicked the ball high between

Hacker and I. 'Well, **who wants it?**' he called out.

Hacker and I looked at each other. Then up at the ball.

Then back at each other. His face turned even **meaner**.

I was **determined**.

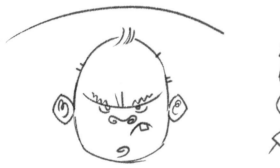

Hacker moved over and positioned himself under

the ball. I'd seen him in games going for headers, and

he would suddenly become **ALL elbows**. I'd have to

watch out for those.

He jumped, ready to head the ball away. He was **big** and **tall** and could jump pretty well for a kid his size. His arms were up and his elbows were out. He looked like a **giant chicken**, flapping its wings.

But he was **no match** for the **spring** in my step!
I took a few paces and **leaped up**, over his
flapping arms, and got my head on the ball above
Hacker's head. I knocked it **straight back** into
Coach Roach's arms!

'Astonishing, Timmy,' said Coach Roach. **'Just astonishing!'**

'He must have got **bionic legs** put in!' said Hacker.

I could hear him talking to Studs after practice. We
were all walking back to class.

'No way,' said Studs. 'That kind of thing costs **lots**
and **lots** of money. **At least $100.**'

'Well, maybe he's put **tiny trampolines** in the bottoms of his boots so he can **bounce up high**,' Hacker suggested. 'How else could he **out-jump** me?!'

'Nup, he just got good and now he can jump really high,' Studs said. 'We knew all along he'd get into the team, maybe even be the **best player**. And now you've let him **beat you** to a header. That's **YOUR thing!**'

'Yeah . . . but would it be so bad if he got in the team?' Hacker asked. 'I mean, he might **help us win**.'

'But **we're the best** players!' Studs said. 'And we need to keep it that way. Get it? We want the kids at school chanting our name, not **Tiny Timmy's**!'

'Best players? **In their dreams**,' Mike scoffed.

But it at least explained why Hacker and Studs had been giving me such a hard time.

They were jealous!

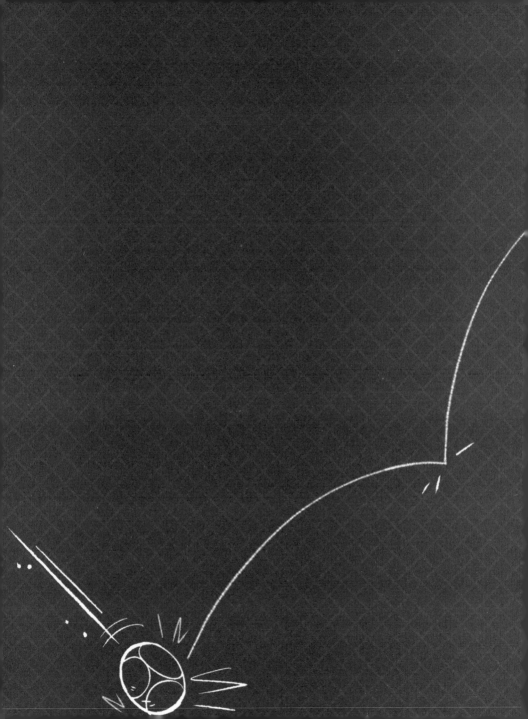

CHAPTER 13

Coach Roach usually posted the T E A M for the next week's game at lunchtime. I was there at the noticeboard as soon as the bell went.

Time went by.

No Coach Roach.

Hacker and Studs walked past.

'Look at **Tiny Timmy**, waiting to see if he's kept his place as **orange boy**,' said Studs.

'Yeah, he should be **dropped**, just like he dropped the oranges last week,' said Hacker.

They couldn't be right, **could they?**

Millie heard Hacker and Studs. 'Don't worry, Tim, we need a player like you. I'm sure Coach Roach will put you on the team,' she said. I really **hoped** *she* was right!

Just when it was time for the bell to go for the end of lunch, I saw Coach Roach walking along the corridor.

'Ah, Timmy! Been **waiting** to see if you've made the side?' he said. 'It took a little longer this time. I was trying to find a way to fit you **into the TEAM**.'

He posted the team sheet on the noticeboard and walked off.

What did that mean? Did he find a way?

Was I <u>in</u> or <u>out</u>?!

I checked the sheet, from the top. **Goalkeeper**, **defenders**—no, they weren't the positions I played.

LIONS' GAME DAY TEAM

```
Goalkeeper:      Liam
Defenders:       Studs
                 Hacker
                 Jonas
                 Sienna
```

I thought my **best position** would be **midfield**, so I held my breath and looked at the names:

```
Midfielders:     Millie
                 Nico
                 Mike
```

and Ti . . . bor. Tibor, not Timmy!

```
Midfielders:     Millie
                 Nico
                 Mike
                 Tibor  ⬅
```

OK, maybe Coach Roach had picked me up front as a **striker**. I could score goals with my feet and my head, so why not? I checked the names, but **I wasn't there**, either!

```
Forwards:        Ibrahim
                 Cruz
```

I had worked **SO hard**, I could **jump higher** than everyone, and it had **all been for NOTHING!**

I looked down the list to see if I had at least kept my place as orange boy, but my name wasn't there, either. This was a **real <u>disaster!</u>**

Just then, Mike walked by on his way to the classroom. He looked at the list.

'Wow, Tim, **congratulations!**' he said. 'A place on the bench. Coach Roach has picked you as an **impact sub!**'

He was right! There was **MY NAME**, one of the **reserves**.

```
Reserves:        Evie
                 Tim
                 Kash
```

Now I'd be able to show everyone what I could do! As long as I had a chance to get on the field . . .

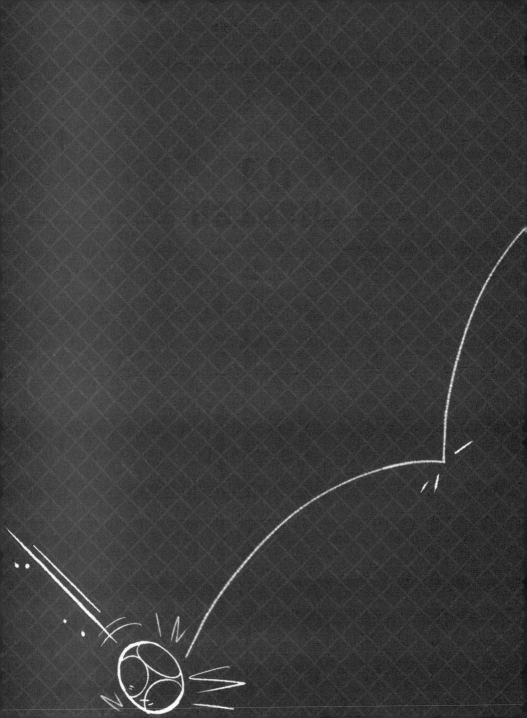

CHAPTER 14

It was the day of the game. I arrived at the field **extra early** with Dad and Mum and Kyah and Shae. I couldn't wait to get out there for my **first proper match!**

All week I'd been practising **harder** than ever. Shae only had to go next door to get the ball once, and that was when Kyah tipped a shot over the clothesline. I was **feeling good**.

We were playing the

ROVERS, who were a good

team—they'd probably make

the finals. It felt great to be

on the bench wearing the

blue **LIONS'** kit for

the first time, but I

was really **hoping**

to get on the pitch

and **play**.

The first half

came and went. **NIL-ALL**. We weren't making many

chances to score, but Hacker and Studs and the rest

of our defence weren't having much trouble, either.

Halfway through the second half, there were still no

goals. It was clear we needed to do something to try

and **shake things up**. Coach Roach looked over to
the bench. This was it. This was **my chance!**

'Evie!' Coach Roach called. 'I'm going to put you

on for Nico. Try

and **unlock that**

defence, lass.'

My heart **sunk**. Here I was, ready
to go, and it looked like I was going to
spend the **entire game** sitting on
the bench.

Another ten minutes passed. There were only five

minutes left! **Give me a CHANCE, Coach Roach!**

And then he did. **'Timmy! You're <u>on</u>!'** He came

over to where I was on the bench. 'I want you to take up a

position in **midfield**, and

if we find some space,

get forward and **join**

the attack.

It'll be just like

I worked out on

my desk with the cola and lemonade.'

I didn't know exactly what he was talking

about, but it sounded **good enough** to me!

'And if you see the ball in the air, lad, use that **leap**

of yours and **get your noggin on it!'** he added.

'We can **win** this!'

As I ran onto the field, I got the feeling that some of the kids and mums and dads who had never seen me play before were **surprised** that I was out there. But then I saw Mum, Dad, Kyah and Shae on the sideline. They knew what I could do, and I wanted to make them **proud**.

There wasn't much time left. I wouldn't have many chances. I'd have to **make the most** of every touch!

I felt nervous. The game was a lot easier when you were **orange boy** . . .

It didn't take long for me to get into the match. Studs made a tackle, collected the ball and kicked it to Mike. Mike looked up and saw that I was **in the clear**. He passed me the ball.

I took it, and . . . passed it back to him. It felt good to take a touch, settle my **nerves** and make the pass.

'Move it forward, **Tiny Timmy**. The goal is that way!' shouted Studs.

'Yeah, the aim of the game is to score goals!' added Hacker.

I made a run towards goal. Mike spotted me and sent a **great** **looping** pass my way.

I jumped up and **collected the ball**, and set off on a  **dribble**.

I **beat a player**,

and **hopped** over

the tackle of another.

It was just like **I'd imagined**.

Now it was just me and the goalkeeper. In my head I could already hear the crowd **chanting** my name.

Tim-my! TIM-MY!

I could **shoot** to the **left**. I could **shoot** to the **right**. I could **lob** the ball over the goalkeeper's head. Maybe I could **shoot between his legs?**

But I didn't get to shoot **at ALL!** One of the defenders had **turned** around, run back, **nudged** me off the ball and **kicked** it away for a **corner**.

I'd taken **TOO long**!

No-one was chanting my name, but I did hear a disappointed '**OOOOOOOH**'.

'Is that *still* the best you can do, **Tiny Timmy**?' said Hacker.

'Yeah, is that *still* all you got?' said Studs.

But a lot **<u>HAD</u> changed** since the tryouts. And now was my chance to prove it!

There wasn't much time left in the match. Mike **rushed to take the corner** before the ref blew his whistle for **FULL-TIME**. I stood at the back post. I heard Studs say to Hacker, 'Get in there and **get the glory**. We need this goal and **we can't trust Tiny Timmy** to win it for us.'

Hacker moved up towards the front post.

The corner kick went straight to Hacker. And

because he was **so big**, the **ROVERS** had him

well covered. I had a tall defender marking me, too.

Maybe word had got around about how

high I could **jump!**

Hacker went full **chicken-flap** with his elbows and j**u**mped **u**p to head the ball in. The players from the other team came from everywhere to stop him getting to it.

Studs yelled out, 'Jump, Hacker! **The glory will be ours!**'

Hacker jumped, but the ball was **too high** and he couldn't get any **≷power≷** on his header. He did manage to get the top of his head to the ball and **flick**  the ball over to the back post, right where **I was waiting**!

≷THIS WAS IT!≷

It seemed like the play was happening in **slow motion**, but really it was over in a **≷flash≷**.

The ball **looped up**.

The defender marking me was in the best position to clear it, and he jumped to head it away. But he didn't jump high enough . . .

I tracked the flight of the ball, timed my run and **sprung up** over the top of their player. **He got the surprise of his life!**

I put my head on the ball. The contact was good, and it ➡ ➡ ➡ **flew towards the top corner** of the goal.

Their keeper **dived**, but he didn't even get a hand

on it! The referee blew the **whistle** for full-time, and I

had scored the **MATCH-WINNING goal!**

I just stood there where I

landed. I didn't have a **goal**

celebration prepared.

I'd have to work on that!

It didn't matter too much, because my teammates

came from everywhere and j**u**mped **ALL over me**.

Well, most of my teammates ...

But I didn't feel <u>a thing</u>!
'Top class, Timmy, TOP
CLASS!' Coach Roach

called from the

sideline.

It *had* all been worth it. I was on my way to

becoming a

Look out for more

**TINY
TIMMY**

books coming soon!